# PANCAKE
## PIE

### by Sven Nordqvist

William Morrow & Company · New York

Library of Congress Cataloging in Publication Data
Nordqvist, Sven. Pancake pie. Translation of: Pannkakstårtan. Summary: Despite many difficulties, a
farmer named Festus is determined to celebrate his cat's birthday by baking a pancake pie. 1. Children's
stories, Swedish. [1. Farm life—Fiction. 2. Cats—Fiction. 3. Pancakes, waffles, etc.—Fiction.
4. Birthdays—Fiction]   I. Title.   PZ7.N7756Pan   1985   [E]   84-16640
ISBN 0-688-04141-8
ISBN 0-688-04142-6 (lib. bdg.)

# PANCAKE
# === PIE ===

There was once a farmer named
Festus who had a cat named Mercury.
They lived in a little red house with a
toolshed, a hen house, a woodshed,
an outhouse, and a garden.
   Mercury had birthdays three times a year,
just because it was more fun that way.
And every time Mercury had a birthday,
Festus baked him a pancake pie.

One birthday morning Festus filled a whole basket with eggs, but he did not start the pancake pie. He sat on the bench outside the kitchen door polishing the eggs. The eggs had to be shiny because Festus liked to do everything the right way.

Mercury paced up and down on the bench. "Do you have to polish all the eggs *now*?" said the cat. "It'll be time for my next birthday before the pie is ready."

"You're so impatient," sighed the farmer. He left the basket
on the bench and took three eggs into the kitchen. Mercury was
already inside looking for the pie pan.

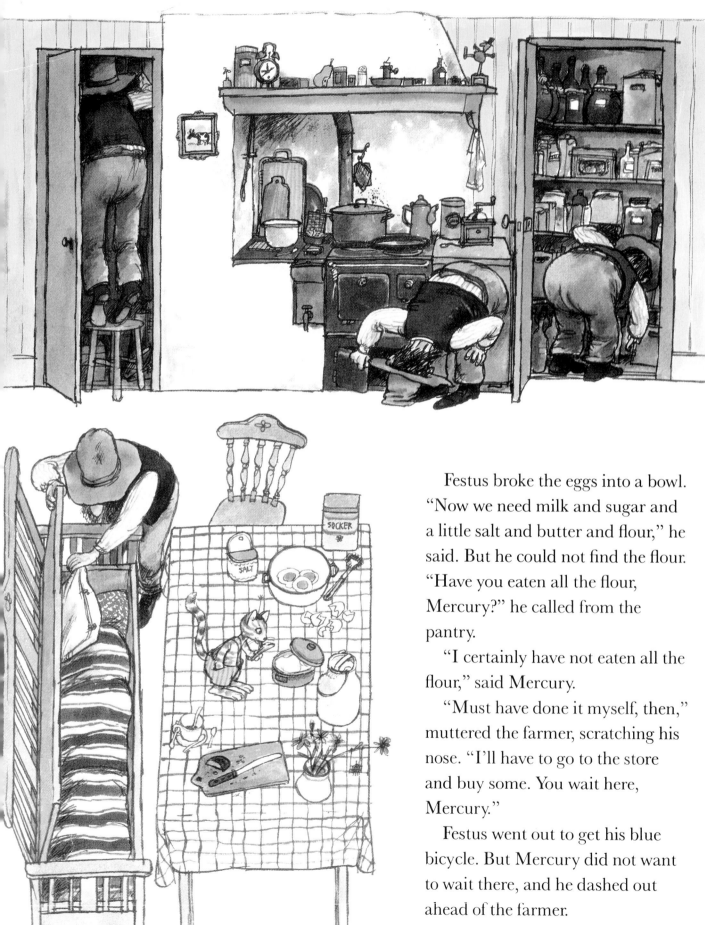

Festus broke the eggs into a bowl. "Now we need milk and sugar and a little salt and butter and flour," he said. But he could not find the flour. "Have you eaten all the flour, Mercury?" he called from the pantry.

"I certainly have not eaten all the flour," said Mercury.

"Must have done it myself, then," muttered the farmer, scratching his nose. "I'll have to go to the store and buy some. You wait here, Mercury."

Festus went out to get his blue bicycle. But Mercury did not want to wait there, and he dashed out ahead of the farmer.

Festus was about to ride off on his bicycle when he noticed that the back tire was flat. "Did you bite a hole in this tire, Mercury?" the farmer grumbled.

"I certainly never bite holes in tires," the cat spat back.

"Must have done it myself, then," mumbled the farmer, pulling his ear. "You wait here, Mercury, and I'll get the bicycle pump from the toolshed. Then I'll fix the tire, go to the store, and buy some flour so we can bake your pancake pie."

But Mercury did not want to wait there, so he ran on ahead.

When Festus got to the toolshed, the door could not be opened, and the key was missing. "Why is this door locked?" the farmer moaned. "Did you lose the key, Mercury?"

"I certainly do not lose keys," Mercury replied.

"Must have done it myself, then," growled the farmer, poking his ear. He peered in through the window of the shed and tried the door again, but it was still locked.

Then he heard Mercury whistle to him from the well. Festus hurried over. "Oh, look, there's the key, right at the bottom," he said. "How did it get there? And how am I going to get it out?"

Festus stared down into the well. "I know! I'll fish the key out. Have you got a long stick, Mercury?"

"I certainly have never had a long stick," said Mercury.

"Must have one myself, then," the farmer said. "Somewhere. You just wait here, Mercury, and I'll go find one. Then I'll fish out the key, open the toolshed, fix the tire, go to the store, and buy some flour so we can bake your pancake pie."

But Mercury did not want to wait there, and he ran on ahead.

Festus and Mercury looked everywhere for a long stick. They looked in the hen house, behind the toolshed, in the garden, in the woodshed, behind the sofa, and in the closet, but they couldn't find a long enough stick anywhere.

Then Festus remembered that he had a fishing pole in the loft above the toolshed. "I'll climb in through the skylight in the roof," he said. "But first I have to get the ladder from behind the woodshed in Hiram's field where his bull is sleeping and using the ladder as a pillow. We'll have to get it away from him. But how?"

Festus thought so hard you could hear his brain ticking.
"Are you any good at bullfighting?" he asked Mercury.
"I certainly have never fought a bull," Mercury gasped.
"Pity," clucked Festus, "because if we can't get the ladder away
from the bull I can't get the fishing rod down from the loft
and get into the toolshed, fix the tire, go to the store, and buy
some flour. And then there'll be no pancake pie for your birthday."

"No pancake pie? Oh, my,"
cried Mercury. "Isn't there
something I can do?"

"Yes, there is. You wait here
and I'll be right back." This
time Mercury waited and
did not run on ahead.

Festus went into the house. He took down one of the flowered kitchen curtains, and he got the old Victrola with the horn. Then he went back outside.

He tied the curtain to Mercury's tail.

"Now you look like a bullfighter in Spain," Festus said.

He put a record on the Victrola and cranked it up. "Hiram's bull won't sleep through this," cackled the farmer. "On your mark, Mercury? Get set. But don't go yet."

When the "Star Spangled Banner" blared out of the Victrola, the bull swiveled around and bellowed. Then he ducked his head, bunched up all his muscles, and thundered toward Festus and Mercury and the Victrola.

"Go!" shouted Festus, and Mercury shot off like a rocket, with the flowered curtain flapping from his tail. The bull took off after the flapping curtain.

Festus crawled under the fence, grabbed the ladder, and got out fast. Three seconds later, Mercury streaked by with the curtain waving behind him. The bull stood panting at the other end of the field, but Mercury kept going anyway.

He whizzed past the bench outside the kitchen door. The curtain caught on the egg basket, flipped it over, and the eggs all rolled into a puddle. Festus, who was right behind, tripped on the curtain and sat down on the eggs.

"Did you leave the eggs on the bench, Mercury?" howled Festus.

"I certainly did not leave any eggs on the bench," Mercury hissed.

"Must have done it myself, then," the farmer hissed back.

Then he calmed down because it was Mercury's birthday. "I'll have to clean up this mess before I bake your pancake pie," he said. "I do like to do things the right way."

Festus took a shovel and started scooping up the muddy, eggy mess. Just then Hiram arrived.

"Hi, neighbor. Working hard as usual, I see," said Hiram.

"Indeed I am," Festus answered. "We're celebrating Mercury's birthday, you see, so I'm making a pancake pie." He emptied the last scoop of eggy mud from the puddle into the bucket and wiped his hands on the seat of his pants. His pants were eggy and sticky, too, so he threw them into the bucket as well.

Hiram's jaw dropped.

"If you only have birthdays three times a year, you should have a real celebration," he told Hiram, pressing the pants down into the bucket.

Hiram just stared at the eggy mud in the bucket.

"It's my own recipe," said Festus proudly. Hiram nodded slowly. "But first I have to go to the store and buy some flour."

Festus took the
ladder over to the
toolshed, climbed up,
and disappeared
over the other side
of the roof.

Hiram stood looking up at the roof for a long time.
Then he looked at the eggy mud in the bucket and at
Mercury pacing back and forth with a flowered curtain
tied to his tail. The Victrola had gotten stuck and was
wailing ". . . home of the brave, brave, brave." Hiram
looked up at the roof again and began walking away as
fast as he could.

Meanwhile Festus had crawled through the skylight into the loft of the toolshed and found the fishing rod. He climbed down again, fastened a hook to the end of the rod, went to the well, and fished out the key. Then he opened the door to the toolshed, fixed the tire, went to the store, bought some flour—and new pants— went home again, and baked a mouthwatering pancake pie for Mercury.

Then Festus and Mercury sat in the garden, eating pancake pie and playing the "Star Spangled Banner" on the old Victrola, just as they always did when Mercury had a birthday.